Return
to
Blueberry Street

TAILS OF BLUEBERRY STREET:

BOOK TWO

To Elijah
A good story is
a real treat!
Debbie Burton

ENDORSEMENTS

It's that charming beagle named Buddy back for more Florida adventures. Debbie Burton has created an engaging character for children that teaches lessons about kindness, teamwork, and conservation. In a child-friendly way, she also addresses the problems of bullying and prejudice—can any cat be trusted? This is a fun book for children and a good book for teachers to complement a unit on Florida wildlife.

—**Mary Alice Archer**, author, *If a Cat*

Debbie Burton has done it again! Our familiar and sweet beagle, Buddy, is off on another adventure that will delight the hearts of young readers everywhere. A true educator, Burton weaves real facts into the storyline, teaching us about Florida and pet-owning while immersing us in the life of our favorite dog and his friends. A joy to read and a must for teachers and parents.

—**Tez Brooks**, writer's coach and award-winning author, *The Single Dad Detour: Directions for Fathering After Divorce.*

Florida author Debbie Burton has brought our beloved friend Buddy the Beagle back for more fun with some added Florida history. *Return to Blueberry Street* brings the adopted beagle and his neighborhood pals to life, including an old bully from her previous book. Students love to hear Buddy's inner voice and curiosity as he studies his humans, Jen and Henry. An added bonus are the questions at the end of the book that make great extension activities in writing, science, and citizenship. This book is a great addition to any classroom, school, or home library.

—**Jennifer Abel**, third-grade teacher, Kennedy Elementary, Manistee Area Public Schools, MI

Our former teacher turned author, Debbie Burton, is back with another story featuring our favorite beagle friend, Buddy. I know children will enjoy reading about his latest adventure. Buddy is engaged as a super-sleuth who must solve the mystery of disappearing packages in the neighborhood. Who could be stealing the dog treats? Buddy is hot on the case. Let's hope this is one of many mysteries Buddy will solve in the future.

—**Dr. Randall Hart,** Principal of Dover Shores Elementary School, Orlando, FL

Buddy the Beagle is back with an important mystery to solve in a story of true friendship and teamwork. Debbie Burton does an excellent job integrating science into a character-driven story kids and adults alike will enjoy. Buddy shows us all that utilizing our strengths and working with friends that look different from us can solve life's biggest challenges. A story of curiosity, compassion, and dogged determination.

—**Arielle Haughee**, children's book editor, author, *Grumbler*

Return
to
Blueberry Street

TAILS OF BLUEBERRY STREET
BOOK TWO

DEBBIE BURTON

ELK LAKE PUBLISHING INC
Plymouth, Massachusetts
PUBLISHING THE POSITIVE

Cover and Interior Design: Derinda Babcock
Illustrator: Mickey Leonard
Editor(s): Bobbie Temple, Deb Haggerty
Author Represented By: WordWise Media Services

PUBLISHED BY: Elk Lake Publishing, Inc., 35 Dogwood Drive, Plymouth, MA 02360, 2020

Library Cataloging Data
Names: Burton, Debbie (Debbie Burton)
Return to Blueberry Street Tails of Blueberry Street Book Two / Debbie Burton
74 p. 21.6 cm × 14 cm (8.5 in x 5.5 in.)
Identifiers: ISBN-13: 978-1-64949-047-6 (paperback) |
978-1-64949-048-3 (trade hardcover) | 978-1-64949-049-0 (trade paperback) | 978-1-64949-050-6 (e-book)
Key Words: teamwork; bullies; thieves; rescue dogs; friendship; family, Ages 8-10
LCCN: 2020944194 Fiction

DEDICATION

In memory of my father, who loved to camp in the woods.

ACKNOWLEDGMENTS

Behind every author is a community of people who have contributed to the work. I wish to thank the following for their helpful encouragement and assistance.

Herb Burton
Word Weavers Orlando
Sherri Stewart, Stewart Writing
Mickey Leonard, Mickleo Illustrations
Michelle S. Lazurek, WordWise Media Services
Deb Haggerty, Elk Lake Publishing, Inc.
Derinda Babcock, Elk Lake Publishing, Inc.
Bobbi Temple, Elk Lake Publishing, Inc.

TABLE OF CONTENTS

CHAPTER ONE

The Family Doghouse

Buddy the beagle woke from his nap. *How can a dog sleep around here? Jen is very noisy in the kitchen.*

Henry carried a big bag into the room. "Are you ready, Jen? I've loaded our gear into the car."

"I've packed the soup, crackers, and marshmallows. Can you bring the cooler from the garage?"

"Sure." Henry walked past Buddy's bed and opened the back door.

Buddy perked up. *Are we going for a car ride?*

Jen opened the refrigerator. "Where are the hot dogs? I know I bought some at the store."

Buddy sprang out of bed and pawed at the gate of his pen. *Did you say dog? I'm over here.*

Henry rushed back inside with the cooler. "I can't wait to see Sapphire Springs. Now that we've retired from our jobs, we can leave the city to enjoy nature."

"I found the hot dogs for our trip. Buddy will love camping and hiking through the woods with us."

The little beagle cocked his head. *I heard my name, but I don't know why. I wish I could speak human.*

"I almost forgot. Buddy will need to eat too." Henry carried the large bag of dog food outside.

Buddy whined. *I'm hungry. You're taking my food away. Please, let me out of here.*

When Henry came back, he opened the gate to the dog pen. Buddy rushed out and pranced around the kitchen. *Are we going outside?*

Henry patted Buddy's head. "Stay in the kitchen." He folded the dog pen. "I'll come back to get your bed."

Buddy ran to his bed and climbed in. *No way. Not without me. If the bed goes, I go.*

Jen held a treat for Buddy to sniff. *M-m-m, Yummy Treats.* Buddy gobbled the treat from her hand. "I've got you, little guy. You're coming with me."

Jen secured Buddy inside his travel crate. Henry stacked the dog bed on top of all the supplies in the back of the jeep. Finally, the little family started their trip.

Buddy sighed. *Whew. For a minute I thought I wasn't coming.*

Jen clicked her seat belt. "Are you nervous about pulling the trailer behind the jeep?"

"I'm a little nervous. This is our first trip and we have much to learn. Do you hear the rattling sound? Our trailer is noisy rolling down the road."

The rattling sound lulled Buddy asleep. He stirred when Jen raised her voice. "Look, a deer by the road."

Henry pressed the brakes. "We don't want to hit the deer. I'm glad the doe ran back into the woods."

Buddy whined from the back of the car. *What's going on?*

"We've entered the park and we're already seeing Florida wildlife." Jen turned around in her seat. "Hang on, Buddy. We're almost to the campsite."

Henry drove farther. "Look at the beautiful live oaks along the side of the road. I imagine these trees are a hundred years old."

The jeep slowed again. "Here's our campsite," said Henry. "Will you get out and direct me while I back the trailer in?"

Jen hopped out of the jeep. Henry parked the trailer and walked around to lift the back gate. "We're here."

Buddy stood and wagged his tail. *I'm ready!*

Henry attached the leash to Buddy's harness and they walked the grounds. Buddy sniffed the trees and plants along the dirt road. *I smell many new things. I detect squirrels and dogs, but the other scents are new to me.*

Back at the campsite, Buddy cocked his head. *Where's Jen?*

Henry held Buddy as he opened the door to the trailer. "Jen, can you watch Buddy? I'll build the campfire."

"I'd love to. Welcome to our travel home, little guy."

The nosy beagle sniffed around their tiny one-room home. *I love this new place. Jen fits here too. I've always wanted a family doghouse.*

Jen hummed a tune as she prepared dinner. Buddy stayed close to her feet. *Maybe she'll drop a morsel of food.*

Soon, Henry opened the door and picked Buddy up. He carried him outside to his pen where his soft bed waited for him. "Here you go, my furry friend. Enjoy the great outdoors."

Buddy stood still and stared into the dark woods. *What are those strange noises? I'm scared.*

Henry lit the firewood. Soon, the flames brightened the campsite. The wood crackled and popped.

Jen placed two mugs on the picnic table. "Dinner's ready."

Henry joined her. "Hot soup is perfect for a cool night."

"I love watching a campfire on nights like this." Jen sipped her soup. "Buddy looks worried. He's not in his bed."

"Oh, I remember. He needs to eat." Henry hurried into the trailer and returned with Buddy's dish. "Here, pal. Eat your dinner."

Buddy gobbled his food and crawled into his comfortable bed. *Ah ... tastes like home.*

Jen looked toward the woods. "Do you hear something moving in the leaves?"

Buddy stood. *I hear something. Outdoor life is noisy.*

Henry turned on a flashlight and scanned the campsite. "Look, I see two tiny ears and a pointy snout."

"Oh, I see an armadillo. They like to dig for food under the fallen leaves. Don't worry, the busy guy won't bother us." Jen returned to her chair by the fire. Buddy laid back in his bed. *Thanks, Jen. I can relax now.*

The flames burned lower. Jen stood up and rubbed her hands together. "The night air is chilly. Let's go to bed. I'm tired."

"The fire is almost out. We should go in." Henry lifted Buddy and followed Jen to the trailer.

Buddy curled up on a blanket under the dinette table. *I can't believe we're sleeping in the same room. I like our cozy family doghouse. Sweet dreams, everyone.*

CHAPTER TWO

The Hike to Sapphire Springs

Buddy squirmed on the picnic table. *Oh no, must I wear the booties?*

Henry tugged the red boots on to Buddy's back feet and lowered him to the ground. "Now, you're ready."

The little beagle pulled on his leash. *Let's go!*

Jen laced up her sneakers and the family began their walk. At the end of the road, they paused in front of a big sign.

Jen read out loud. "'Sapphire Springs Trailhead. Three miles round trip.' I'm glad Buddy has booties. They'll protect his back feet on our long hike."

Buddy saw a boy and his mother walk out of the woods. The little boy pointed. "Look, the doggy has red shoes."

Jen greeted the boy. "I'm Jen and this is Buddy. He hurt his back a year ago. He couldn't move his hind legs, but now he can walk again. Sometimes he drags his feet, but the booties prevent sores."

The boy looked up at Jen. "Can I pet him?"

"Sure. Buddy likes children."

The child stroked the little beagle's fur. "His ears feel like velvet. Oh, he gave me a doggy kiss."

Henry pulled Buddy away. "I'm sorry."

What's the matter, Henry? I like meeting new friends.

The mother patted Buddy. "We don't mind at all. We love dogs. Thanks for the kiss, Buddy." She took her child's hand and walked toward the campground.

Jen returned to the Sapphire Springs sign. "Someone snapped a photo of a monkey who lives in this park."

Henry and Buddy looked closer. Buddy cocked his head. *A monkey? I've never seen a monkey before.*

Jen read more. "'Beware of monkeys in the area. Do not approach or feed. Keep your pet leashed at all times.'"

Henry tightened his grip on Buddy's leash. "I didn't know monkeys live in Florida."

A ranger walked up behind them. "I'm afraid so. In the 1930s, a man brought six rhesus monkeys here from Asia. He put the monkeys on an island in the middle of the Sapphire River for boaters to see. Imagine his surprise when he learned the monkeys could swim. They swam to shore and made their home in the woods."

Jen looked at Buddy. "How many monkeys live here now? Are they dangerous?"

"We think we have around two hundred monkeys. When people feed them, they lose their fear of humans. They won't bother you if you don't bother them. But keep your beagle close."

Henry nodded. "Yes, sir. We will."

The family walked to the beginning of the trail. Buddy charged forward with his nose to the sandy ground. *I'm excited! Sniff-sniff. I think I smell monkeys.*

Henry gripped the leash but let Buddy forge ahead. The little beagle looked back to make sure everyone had followed him. *Hurry, Jen. Why are you walking so slow?*

Henry noticed. "Buddy thinks he's the lead dog, and we're part of his pack."

Haven't you heard of the buddy system? The little beagle sighed.

As they rounded the bend in the trail, Henry stepped onto a boardwalk. "Look, we're crossing over a swamp. I'm glad we don't have to walk through the green water."

"Me too." Jen peered across the wetland. "The swamp looks murky. Who knows what kind of creatures swim under the surface."

Henry pointed at the knobby knees of the bald cypress trees. "I've seen these before. The cone-like shapes are part of the bald cypress root system. They fix the tree into the soft mud and support the trunk."

Buddy leaned over the edge of the boardwalk to see the swamp. *I don't see any monkeys.*

Henry pulled him away. "Back up, Buddy! You don't want a gator to eat you for lunch."

Buddy cocked his head. *Henry seems alarmed. Does something scary live in the water?*

Jen pulled a trail map from her pocket. "The river runs close to the swamp. Let's keep going."

Jen reached the dock first. "Look at the beautiful Sapphire River. I can see schools of tiny fish in the clear water."

Henry came alongside and peered down to the bottom. "The river flows out of Florida's aquifer, deep underground."

Buddy looked up at Henry. *How can we cross the river? You know I hate baths.*

"Look, I see a kayak." Henry waved at two teenage boys paddling to shore.

10

Buddy stepped closer to greet the boys, but they raced into the woods without noticing him. The little beagle cocked his head. *Hey, don't you want to play with me?*

Jen watched the boys as they vanished behind the trees. "I wonder why they ran?"

Henry shrugged. "I have no idea. But we must return to our campsite. I see clouds moving in, the wind is picking up, and there's a storm brewing."

Buddy pulled on his leash. *I smell something good.*

Henry grasped the leash tighter. "Uh-oh, I think Buddy found a scent. He's on the move."

Jen zipped up her jacket. "At least he's going in the right direction. Let's hurry."

Buddy led Henry and Jen across the swamp to the end of the boardwalk. His nose led the way along the sandy trail through the oaks. *I must find the source of the smell.* Then, he froze in his tracks. *I found something!*

Henry picked up a banana peel from the middle of the trail. "Somebody did not throw their trash away."

Buddy pulled Henry again.

A new sound echoed from the trees ahead. "Eek-eek."

Jen slowed her pace. "I hear a monkey. Keep a tight hold on Buddy."

Just around the bend, they met the two boys from the river. One boy offered a banana to the tiny monkey on the trail. The other boy held a net and hid behind a tree.

The baby monkey crept toward the banana. His mama screeched from the tree limbs above, "FREDDY, COME BACK! THOSE BOYS WANT TO CATCH YOU."

Buddy barked, "STOP!"

The little monkey looked at Buddy. "ARE YOU TALKING TO ME?"

Buddy barked again. "YOU NEED TO TURN AROUND AND GO BACK. DON'T TRUST THEM."

The baby monkey stepped away from the boys. His mother rushed down from the tree and scooped him up. She placed him on her back and climbed to the top of a tree.

Thunder boomed. The boy dropped the banana on the ground. "We'd better get out of here. I don't like storms or dogs!" The two boys hurried toward the river.

Buddy used his mouth to carry the banana to Henry.

Henry traded a treat for the banana. "Good boy, Buddy."

The mama monkey cuddled her baby and cooed. "THANK YOU FOR SAVING FREDDY. I TELL HIM TO STAY AWAY FROM PEOPLE, BUT HE LOVES TO EAT. YOU CAME AT THE RIGHT TIME, BUDDY."

The little beagle yipped, "FREDDY IS LIKE ME. I LIKE TO EAT TOO."

Jen snapped a photo of the two monkeys. "I can't believe monkeys live in Sapphire Springs."

Thunder boomed closer this time.

"Let's go!" Henry snatched Buddy and ran back to the campground. Jen jogged behind them.

They arrived at the trailer as the storm hit. Safely inside, Henry pulled the banana from his pocket. "Let's have fruit salad for lunch."

Buddy looked at Henry. *What about me? What do I get?*

"How about a Yummy Treat, little guy? Here you go."

Buddy gobbled the morsel. *I love Yummy Treats.*

Jen turned to Henry. "Why do you think those boys wanted to catch the little monkey?"

Henry sighed. "Maybe they wanted to keep him. Monkeys need special care to stay healthy and they are hard to train. Some people forget wild monkeys do not make good house pets like cats and dogs."

"But we know beagles make the best house pets." Jen tossed Buddy another treat.

Give me Yummy Treats and I will obey your rules.
Buddy smiled his doggy smile.

CHAPTER THREE

Fair Play at the Dog Park

Back home on Blueberry Street, Henry scooped dry dog food into Buddy's bowl. The little beagle shuffled with excitement and yipped. *Come on, Henry! Give me my kibble.*

Henry carefully placed the bowl in front of Buddy. Their eyes met. "Okay, you can eat."

Buddy gobbled his breakfast in one minute, then licked his lips. *Can I have more?*

Jen looked up from her bowl of cereal. "Buddy eats so fast. How can he taste his food?"

"He ate the food in one gulp. Maybe he enjoys the flavor of the food as he swallows."

Buddy walked under the table and sniffed around Jen's feet. *What are you having for breakfast?*

Jen reached down to pat him. "Are you looking for more food to eat? I bet you could gobble a whole bag of dog food in one sitting."

Henry sipped his coffee. "Beagles can gain weight if their owners aren't careful. Buddy exercised a lot on our camping trip, but he's not very active at home. We should take him to the dog park today."

When Buddy heard "dog park," he pawed at the door. Then, he rushed back and looked up at Henry. *What are you waiting for? I'm ready.*

Jen opened the gate to the dog park. "Look. In the area reserved for small dogs, I see a beagle. Let's go."

Once inside the small-dog zone, Henry released Buddy from his leash. An older beagle greeted him. "Hi, Bandit. Remember me?"

Buddy sniffed the beagle's neck. "Max! I remember you from the beagle rescue. How did you end up here?"

"The nice man sitting on the bench adopted me. His name is Charlie. I see you're with the same family. Good job. They must love you," yipped Max.

"I had a hard time with their rules, but I've learned how much I need them. By the way, they changed my name right after I moved in. I'm Buddy now."

"Buddy? You don't say. Well, I'm still Max. I see something different about you. What's with the red booties?"

"Two years ago, I jumped off the bed and hurt my back. I had to go to the animal hospital. I couldn't walk for a long time. I'm better, but I can't run or jump anymore. Jen insists I wear these silly boots to protect my feet. Are you still my friend?"

Max wagged his tail. "Of course, I'm still your friend. Don't worry about your feet. I'm not as fast anymore either."

Buddy lowered his head. "Some dogs make fun of me and call me names."

"SOME DOGS NEED SPECIAL TRAINING TO LEARN FRIENDSHIP," Max woofed.

The two beagles played in the yard while Henry and Jen talked with Charlie. Henry called, "Come, Buddy."

Both beagles toddled to the bench. "Hi, Buddy," Charlie said. "Nice to meet you."

Charlie let Buddy sniff him before petting him on the head. Max squeezed in and Buddy moved over. "Yes, Max. You deserve a pat, too." Charlie fastened the leash to Max's collar. "I can't believe we both live in the same neighborhood and haven't run into each other before today. I'd like to stay longer, but we must get home."

Max turned toward Buddy. "WAIT, LET ME SNIFF YOU BEFORE I GO."

Buddy wagged his tail. "I'LL SNIFF YOU BACK."

Henry and Charlie said their goodbyes. Buddy watched Max leave. *I hope I'll see Max again.*

Suddenly, a loud bark came from outside the fence. Buddy's hair pricked up. He stared at another dog from the neighborhood, a big Doberman named Blitz.

Blitz teased Buddy. "I SEE THE BABY BEAGLE WITH THE RED SHOES HAS VISITED THE DOG PARK TODAY. WHY DON'T YOU COME OUT OF THE NURSERY AND RACE WITH THE BIG DOGS?"

Buddy barked back. "THANK YOU, BUT I'M FINE WHERE I AM."

"OH, I SEE. YOU CAN'T RUN ANYMORE," Blitz snapped.

"Stop, Blitz. Be nice." Doug strode to the fence. "Hi, Henry. I haven't seen you and Buddy around lately."

"We went camping at Sapphire Springs. Did you know wild monkeys live in the park?" Henry turned toward Jen. "Show Doug the picture you snapped."

Doug leaned over the fence to look. "Awesome. Nice picture."

Jen pointed at the photo. "Buddy saved this monkey from danger. We saw two boys using a banana to lure the baby into their net. As the baby monkey stepped closer to their trap, Buddy barked and scared the boys away."

"I'm proud of him." Doug reached into his pocket. "Do you mind if I give Buddy a treat? He deserves a reward."

"Okay," Henry said. "But only one treat. We're trying to control his weight."

Buddy gobbled the biscuit. *Yummy.*

Blitz pawed the fence and growled, "WHERE'S MY TREAT?"

Buddy barked, "SORRY, BLITZ. HAVE YOU BEEN A GOOD BOY LATELY?"

Doug clicked Blitz's leash in place. "Come on, big guy. You need a bath."

"Not fair!" Blitz barked. "BUDDY GETS A TREAT AND I GET A YUCKY BATH."

Buddy wagged his tail. "DON'T WORRY, BLITZ. IF YOU BEHAVE, YOU WILL GET A TREAT TOO."

CHAPTER FOUR

The Case of the Missing Yummy Treats

Henry opened and closed the front door. He walked into the kitchen to pour himself some coffee. "I don't understand what happened. I ordered more Yummy Treats for Buddy. The package should have arrived yesterday. The postman left nothing in the mailbox and nothing on the porch."

Buddy cocked his head. *Where are my Yummy Treats?*

Jen glanced up from her book. "Maybe the postman left the treats at a different house number. A house on this street uses the same numbers in their address. We should visit them and ask if they know anything."

Henry nodded. "Good idea. Next time we walk Buddy, we will stop by."

In the afternoon, Buddy strolled down Blueberry Street with Henry and Jen. She pointed toward a house and read the address out loud. "See, the number is 342. Our house number is 324."

"Here, you take Buddy." Henry handed her the leash. "I'll go up and knock on the door."

Henry knocked three times and waited. A dog barked.

Buddy cocked his head. *Another dog. I like our street.*

A lady opened the door a crack. "Willie, not so fast!" A long brown dachshund wiggled through the tight opening.

Buddy barged up the porch steps. Henry raised his voice, "Buddy, no one invited you up here."

The lady stepped onto the porch. "Don't worry. Your little beagle looks harmless."

Buddy approached the dachshund and sniffed. "I'M BUDDY. YOU HAVE A LONG BODY, JUST LIKE ME."

The little dachshund wiggled side to side. "I'M WILLIE. MY LEGS ARE SHORTER THAN YOURS, BUT DON'T BE FOOLED. I CAN RUN FAST."

"I RAN FAST ONCE." Buddy wagged his tail. "I CAN'T RACE ANYMORE, BUT I'M STILL GOOD AT SNIFFING. YOU SMELL LIKE A FRIEND."

"Oh, look. Our pets get along well." Henry reached out to shake the lady's hand. "I'm Henry. This is my wife, Jen, and our beagle, Buddy. We live down the street at 324."

"Nice to meet you. My name's Anne. Yes, beagles and dachshunds are alike. They both like to hunt. I must watch this one. He'll follow his nose anywhere."

Jen nodded. "I know what you mean. Buddy favors smelling and eating. We ordered a package of Yummy Treats, which never arrived yesterday. We wondered if the postman confused our address with yours?"

Anne shook her head. "If I had received your mail by mistake, I would have stopped by your house. Last week, I heard a local news report about people missing packages on the north side of town. Do you suppose a bandit stole your delivery from your front porch?"

"I hope not." Jen looked down at Buddy and Willie. "We might need to get our hunting dogs on the case. I'm sure they could catch the bandit."

Buddy cocked his head. *Bandit? My old name was Bandit, but Henry changed my name to Buddy. Humans confuse me.*

A few days later, Henry and Jen took Buddy to the small-dog zone at the park. Buddy wagged his tail and howled, "Max! Willie! I'm so happy to see you."

Once inside the fence, Henry unhooked Buddy's leash. He and Jen joined their neighbors at the picnic table. The three little dogs roamed around the yard. A loud bark interrupted them, and Buddy stopped in his tracks.

Blitz pressed his nose against the chain-link fence to tease him. "LOOKS LIKE A BUSY DAY IN PUPPY PRE-K. I SEE YOU HAVE SOME NEW BABY FRIENDS."

Buddy stepped closer to the fence and barked, "MAX AND WILLIE ARE NOT BABIES."

The two small dogs came alongside him. Max panted, "YOU OKAY, BUDDY?"

Buddy wagged his tail. "YES, MAX. I'M FINE."

Blitz turned his head toward Max. "YOU LOOK MUCH OLDER THAN THE OTHER TWO. WHY ARE YOU HANGING OUT WITH A CRYBABY BEAGLE AND HIS LOW-TO-THE-GROUND SIDEKICK?"

Max barked back, "BUDDY AND I HAVE KNOWN EACH OTHER A LONG TIME. HE'S MY FRIEND."

Blitz snarled, "YOU DON'T KNOW BUDDY. HE ACTS LIKE A GOOD DOG, BUT I'VE SEEN HIS DARK SIDE."

Doug whistled from across the park. Blitz bolted to meet him.

Max stepped closer to Buddy. "WHY DOES HE BULLY YOU?"

Buddy lowered his head. "MY PROBLEMS WITH BLITZ BEGAN AT THE DOGGY DERBY TWO YEARS AGO. HE CAN'T GET OVER A SPAT WE HAD ABOUT POPCORN. I SPIED SOME KERNELS LEFT ON THE GROUND. I GOBBLED THE SNACK BEFORE HE DID. HE THINKS I STOLE HIS POPCORN FROM HIM. HE WON'T FORGIVE ME, EVEN THOUGH I SAID I'M SORRY."

"DON'T LET BLITZ GET YOU DOWN. I'LL STAND BY YOU," Max yelped.

Willie barked, "DID BLITZ CALL ME A NAME? NOT NICE."

The three dogs joined their humans at the picnic table.

"What are we going to do about this problem?" Charlie asked. "The dog treats I ordered for Max are missing. The post office told me the package had been delivered."

Henry peered at Buddy. "We're missing our treats too. They cost less when we order them through the mail. Yummy Treats makes Buddy's favorite salmon flavor."

Anne patted her dachshund. "My Willie likes the bacon flavor. I think a thief has stolen our parcels."

Henry clipped Buddy's leash into place. "Well, the bold bandit takes things in broad daylight. As neighbors, we should stay alert when we walk our dogs. We might catch the crook."

Buddy wagged his tail. *Are you talking about my Yummy Treats?* He sniffed under the picnic table. *How strange. I smell a monkey.*

CHAPTER FIVE

The Challenge

Henry and Buddy shuffled toward Willy's house. Buddy's nose took over. Sniff, sniff. *I smell a monkey again.* The little beagle led Henry to a grassy lot.

Henry scanned the overgrown yard. "What's going on, Bud? I need to check for any garbage you might gobble."

Buddy stopped at the base of a tall tree and looked up. "FREDDY!"

The little monkey chattered, "I REMEMBER YOU. YOU'RE BUDDY, THE DOG WHO HELPED ME IN THE FOREST. MY MOM LIKED YOU. I'D KNOW YOU ANYWHERE BECAUSE OF YOUR RED BOOTS."

Buddy barked, "NO ONE COULD FORGET THESE BOOTS. HOW DID YOU GET HERE?"

"I'M LOST. HAVE YOU SEEN MY MAMA? WE LEFT THE WOODS TO FIND FOOD."

Henry pulled hard on Buddy's leash. "Let's go. You shouldn't get too close. You can't trust a wild monkey."

Buddy stalled. *I don't want to leave. Freddy needs help.*

Henry picked Buddy up and carried him toward home.

The little beagle whined. "SORRY, FREDDY. TIME TO GO."

When they reached a safe distance away, Henry placed Buddy back on the sidewalk, keeping a tight grip on his leash. "Listen, little guy. You need to obey. The ranger at Sapphire Springs said we must stay away from wild monkeys."

Did I do something bad? You liked when I barked and scared the boys away.

Buddy plodded along with his nose to the ground. He lunged into the bushes before Henry could stop him.

"Now what do you have?" Henry pulled plastic from Buddy's mouth. "How did a Yummy Treats wrapper get here?"

Buddy lowered his head. *Just my luck. The bag is empty.*

"Come on, Buddy." Henry hurried into the front door of their home.

"Jen, you're not going to believe this."

Jen bounded down the stairs to the foyer. "Believe what?"

"Buddy and I met a baby monkey in the vacant lot down the street."

"A monkey on our street? Impossible."

"Buddy took me right to him. What an amazing nose he has!"

The little beagle wagged his tail. *I saw Freddy. Remember Freddy?*

Later, the people who lived on Blueberry Street met at the dog park. Charlie, Henry, and Anne sat at the picnic table near the fence. Max, Willie, and Buddy huddled by the trees at the far end of the small-dog zone.

"WE SHOULD START OUR OWN DOG CRIME WATCH," Buddy barked. "TODAY, I NOTICED A WRAPPER ON BLUEBERRY STREET. THE EMPTY BAG SMELLED LIKE SALMON YUMMY TREATS. HAVE YOU SEEN ANYTHING STRANGE ON OUR STREET?"

"NOT YET," Willie wiggled side to side, "BUT I'LL STAY ALERT."

"WE MUST DO SOMETHING," Max woofed. "I HAVEN'T EATEN A TREAT FOR DAYS. NO TREATS MIGHT MAKE A GOOD DOG TURN BAD."

"I HAVE MORE TO TELL YOU," Buddy yipped. "I FOUND A WILD MONKEY."

"WHAT'S A WILD MONKEY?" Willie cocked his head.

Buddy spied the area. "THEY ARE FURRY ANIMALS WITH LONG TAILS, AND THEY CLIMB TREES."

Max sniffed the air. "WHAT DO THEY SMELL LIKE? I'VE TRACKED MANY SQUIRRELS ON OUR STREET, BUT I'VE NEVER SEEN A WILD MONKEY."

"THEY SMELL MUSKY, KIND OF GOOD AND BAD AT THE SAME TIME," Buddy barked. "I DON'T THINK WILD MONKEYS TAKE BATHS."

"BOY, ARE THEY LUCKY," Max bayed.

The three dogs trotted near their owners who sat at the picnic table. Doug and Blitz leaned over the fence.

Henry looked up at Doug. "Have you noticed any monkeys around?"

Doug's eyes widened. "Monkeys? How could we have monkeys on Blueberry Street?"

"I'm not kidding," Henry said. "This morning, Buddy led me to the vacant lot. We saw one in a tree."

"Didn't you tell me Buddy rescued a monkey at Sapphire Springs?" Doug asked. "Maybe a troop of wild monkeys followed you home."

Henry stroked his little beagle's fur. "Buddy barked and scared away two boys who tried to catch a baby monkey. I don't think the same monkey followed us. But I think our forests do not have enough space for more baby monkeys. In Florida, people cut down forests to build houses. When wild animals can't find food and shelter, they may move to new places."

Charlie patted Buddy. "You're a good boy for saving the monkey."

Buddy wagged his tail. *I'm a good boy!*

Max yipped. "Buddy, I didn't know you were a hero."

Blitz growled from behind the chain-link fence. "Buddy, a hero? No way."

Max barked, "He's the leader of our dog crime watch. Buddy found a clue today. He found an empty bag of treats."

"Ha!" Blitz snarled. "A leader? Buddy is pulling your tail. I wouldn't follow him anywhere. Only Dobermans can catch criminals. Some of my Doberman friends work with the police."

"Then, why don't you track down the thief?" Buddy barked.

"You're on, Buddy," Blitz howled. "I challenge your phony crime watch to a contest. The first dog to catch the thief earns the title, 'Super Sleuth of Blueberry Street.'"

"I accept your challenge," Buddy yipped.

"What's gotten into our dogs?" Henry asked.

"Something stirred them up. Come here, Max." Charlie stood and fastened Max's leash to his collar.

Henry clicked Buddy's leash into place. "We need to go home too. Let's meet here next Saturday. Maybe our dogs will behave better."

CHAPTER SIX

Bad Dog

Buddy curled up on his favorite floor pillow. *Ah, I had a busy day with Henry and Jen. Time for bed.*

Henry closed his laptop. "I ordered another box of Yummy Treats. The package should arrive tomorrow."

Buddy raised his head. *Treats? Did someone say treats?*

Jen checked her phone. "Are you staying home tomorrow? I go to the hair salon at noon."

Henry nodded. "Buddy and I will sit on the porch and wait for the postman. No bandit will steal our treats this time."

Buddy stood up and walked closer to Henry. *I miss my Yummy Treats, and I will catch whoever tries to steal them.*

Jen grabbed her book from the coffee table. "Don't forget to walk Buddy in the morning."

Henry reached to pat his little beagle on the head. "Hmm … maybe I could put a doggy diaper on him."

I remember diaper. I'm a big boy now. Please don't put a diaper on me. Okay?

The next morning, Henry took Buddy for a walk. The little beagle found a clue in the alley behind the house. *Oh, boy! A trash can fell over. Scraps blew everywhere.*

Buddy lunged forward and snatched something with his mouth.

"Stop!" Henry yanked Buddy back. "Rotten pizza can make you sick."

The little beagle licked the crumbs from his mouth. *Too late. Tastes yummy to me.*

Henry carried Buddy away from the garbage. "Bad dog!"

Buddy sighed. *I'm a bad dog. Max was right. He said good dogs can turn bad if they don't get their treats anymore.*

Henry carried Buddy farther down the alley and placed him on the ground. The little beagle saw a brown tail sneak behind the trash can. *Freddy?*

"Come on." Henry pulled harder on the leash. "We need to get home before the Yummy Treats arrive."

But what about Freddy? He might want yummy food, just like me.

Buddy lowered his head and followed his master home.

Back on the porch, Henry sat in his rocking chair. He looped Buddy's leash to the leg of a small table. "Stay."

Buddy perked his ears. *I hear something.*

Max and Charlie walked up to Henry's porch. "Henry, good to see you. What are you and Buddy doing?"

"We're waiting for the postman to bring Buddy's box of Yummy Treats. The bandit won't get them this time. You're welcome to join us."

Max bounded up the porch steps and sniffed Buddy. "DID YOU FIND ANY MORE CLUES?"

Buddy yipped, "I'M TRYING, BUT HENRY ALWAYS STOPS ME."

"SAME HERE," Max barked. "CHARLIE WON'T LET ME FIND CLUES."

Charlie sat next to the two dogs. "I can't make Max obey me. Last night, he sniffed up and down the alley behind our house. He didn't want to go inside. He acts odd."

Henry peered at Buddy. "My beagle ate pizza crust from the alley trash this morning."

"Aw, do you like pizza, little guy?" Charlie stroked Buddy's soft ears.

Max moved closer. "HEY, BUDDY, HOW CAN WE CATCH THE BANDIT BEFORE BLITZ?"

"MAX, YOU'RE A TRUE FRIEND, BUT I DON'T THINK I CAN CATCH THE BANDIT. I CAN'T RUN ANYMORE."

Max cocked his head. "DON'T WORRY, BUDDY. WITH YOUR NOSE AND MY FEET, WE CAN."

Charlie rose from his seat. "Come, Max. Time to go. Shall we meet for the crime watch tomorrow?"

"Yes, I hope we'll solve this case soon." Henry patted Max on the head. "Thanks for stopping by. You and Max are always welcome here."

Charlie waved from the sidewalk. "I hope you don't miss the postman."

Jen opened the front door and joined them on the porch. "I thought you two might need water."

She passed a bottle to Henry and placed Buddy's bowl on the floor. He lapped the dish dry. *Thanks.*

Henry drank. "I needed water, but I'm hungry too. Will you bring me a sandwich before you go to the salon?"

"Sure." Jen went inside. Soon, she returned with a peanut butter and jelly sandwich.

Buddy moved closer to Henry's feet to catch crumbs.

"Be a good boy." Jen rubbed Buddy's head before she left.

"Sorry, pal. This is my snack." Henry bit his sandwich. "Ow!" He held his hand on his jaw.

Buddy peered up at Henry. *What happened?*

The sandwich fell to the porch floor and Henry raced inside.

The little beagle cocked his head and licked his lips. *Should I?*

Suddenly, a brown, furry animal raced onto the porch. The ball of fur stole Henry's sandwich and left.

Buddy barked. He pulled his leash, still looped around the table leg. *I'm stuck. Did I see Freddy?* Buddy sniffed around the empty plate. *He's a quick little guy.*

Henry returned and untied Buddy. "Sorry, Bud. Come inside with me. No Yummy Treats yet."

Jen met them at the front door. "The dentist wants to see you right away. I told him the nuts in the peanut butter cracked your tooth."

"I can't believe I broke my tooth eating a sandwich." Henry rubbed his jaw. "By the way, what happened to my lunch? Buddy, did you eat my sandwich?"

The little beagle cocked his head. *Henry, I think Freddy stole your snack.*

"First pizza ... now my sandwich. What will we do with you?" Henry put Buddy into his crate.

Jen picked up her keys. "This is awful. We both need to leave. Who will watch for the postman?"

Buddy sighed as Henry and Jen walked out the door. *Oh, no. I'm stuck inside my crate and can't look for clues. How can I help Max and Willie catch the bandit?*

CHAPTER SEVEN

More Clues

The next day, the neighbors went to the dog park for the crime watch meeting. Buddy, Max, and Willie stood near the big tree by the fence.

"WHAT'S UP, GUYS?" Max yipped. "HAVE YOU FOUND MORE CLUES TO HELP SOLVE THE CASE?"

"I SAW FREDDY AGAIN." Buddy made sure Blitz wasn't nearby. "FREDDY IS THE LITTLE MONKEY I MET WHEN WE WENT CAMPING."

Willie wiggled closer. "ARE YOU SURE YOU SAW THE SAME MONKEY?"

Buddy lowered his yip, "FREDDY NABBED A SANDWICH FROM OUR FRONT PORCH AFTER MAX LEFT OUR HOUSE YESTERDAY."

"HE SOUNDS SMART TO ME," Max barked. "YOU COULDN'T STOP HIM?"

"I TRIED, BUT HENRY HAD TIED ME TO A TABLE. I DON'T TRUST FREDDY. HE STOLE MY HUMAN'S FOOD. MAYBE HE'S OUR BANDIT."

Blitz galloped to the fence to bark at Buddy and his friends. "LOOK AT THE LITTLE CANINE CRIME STOPPERS. ALL TALK AND NO ACTION."

Buddy barked back, "WHAT HAVE YOU LEARNED, BLITZ? HAVE YOU SOLVED THE CASE OF THE MISSING TREATS?"

"ALMOST," Blitz yipped. "I'VE GOT MY EYES ON JOJO, THE CAT NEXT DOOR. HER HUMAN LETS HER RUN WITHOUT A LEASH."

"YOU MIGHT BE RIGHT." Willie nodded. "EVERY DOG KNOWS CATS ARE UP TO NO GOOD."

Blitz peered over the fence. "CATS ROAM AROUND WITHOUT THEIR HUMANS WATCHING THEM. I ALSO KNOW JOJO LOVES TO EAT SALMON. I'VE SMELLED THE EMPTY TINS IN THE GARBAGE CAN BEHIND HER HOUSE."

Willie cocked his head. "BUDDY, AREN'T SALMON TREATS YOUR FAVORITE? I KNOW YOU THINK THE BANDIT IS A MONKEY, BUT CATS ARE FURRY ANIMALS. THEY HAVE LONG TAILS LIKE MONKEYS AND CLIMB TREES TOO. MAYBE YOU'RE WRONG."

Blitz howled, "BUDDY THINKS THE BANDIT IS A MONKEY. WHAT A SILLY IDEA. MONKEYS DON'T LIVE ON BLUEBERRY STREET. THEY LIVE IN THE JUNGLE. YOU PUPPY DOGS FOLLOW THE WRONG LEADER. YOU SHOULD WATCH JOJO." Blitz ran off to play with the big dogs near the lake.

Willie cocked his head. "BLITZ HAS A POINT. MAYBE OUR BANDIT IS A CAT." The little dachshund ran to the edge of the small-dog zone and watched the big dogs through the chain-link fence.

Buddy sniffed the ground. "LOOKS LIKE WILLIE AGREES WITH BLITZ. I'VE NEVER MET JOJO BEFORE. MAYBE I'M WRONG. WILL YOU STILL HELP ME?"

Max yipped, "I BELIEVE IN YOU, BUDDY. WE MUST KEEP TRYING. DON'T GIVE UP."

Buddy wagged his tail. "DON'T GIVE UP. I HEARD THOSE WORDS FROM A PRETTY BEAGLE NAMED DAISY. I MET HER AT THE ANIMAL HOSPITAL. IF DAISY DIDN'T HELP ME, I MIGHT HAVE STOPPED TRYING TO WALK. THANKS, MAX. YOU KNOW HOW TO CHEER UP A FRIEND."

The two beagles ambled toward the nearest tree. They sniffed the ground. "Do you smell what I smell?" Buddy barked.

Max wagged his tail. "Look, I see an empty treat box."

"I'll show Henry." Buddy snatched the box with his mouth.

Both dogs trotted to the picnic table.

"What's in your mouth, little guy?" Henry took the empty box from Buddy's mouth. "Look at this. My name and address are on the outside. I see you found another clue. Good boy."

Buddy wagged his tail. *I'm glad I'm good again.*

"May I look?" Anne reached for the box. "This was shipped two days ago."

Henry nodded. "I wish I'd had these treats yesterday. Too bad we weren't home."

Anne lifted her gaze and scanned the park. "Maybe our bandit was here. He or she could have sat at this table. What a scary thought."

Henry's eyes opened wide. "Do you think the bandit is a dog owner? Would someone who loves dogs steal their treats?"

CHAPTER EIGHT

Blitz Stirs Up Trouble

"Let's go, boy. We have work to do." Henry and Buddy began their walk down Blueberry Street.

Buddy kept his nose to the ground. Sniff, sniff. *So far, no strange scents.*

When they turned the corner, they met a lady peering under her hedges. "Here, JoJo, come to Mama." The lady glanced up at Henry. "Have you seen my calico cat? I often let JoJo out at night. This morning she didn't come home."

Buddy sighed. *JoJo went missing? Hmm …*

Henry looked around. "I haven't seen her, but we have a problem too. Someone stole Buddy's Yummy Treats. We want to find the thief. If we see JoJo, I can call you."

"I'm Jane. You can call me at this number." She handed Henry a card. "I've had JoJo since she was a kitten."

Buddy and Henry stepped into the alley behind Jane's house. Buddy sniffed the pavement and tracked a scent.

"Did you find a scent, boy?" Henry let his little beagle lead him down the alley.

Buddy froze at the base of a tree. He looked up and started to bark. "JoJo!"

"Good boy! I knew if any dog could find her, you would." Henry cheered.

Buddy barked again. "JoJo, WHAT ARE YOU DOING IN THE TREE?"

The scared cat clung to the highest limb. "I'M AFRAID. A BIG DOBERMAN CHASED ME UP HERE EARLY THIS MORNING. HE HAD YELLOW EYES AND BIG TEETH. HE CALLED ME A BANDIT AND TOLD ME HE WOULD HURT ME IF I CAME DOWN. I DIDN'T STEAL FROM ANYONE."

Buddy yipped, "YOU CAN COME DOWN NOW. YOU'RE SAFE. THE DOBERMAN LEFT."

"ARE YOU SURE?" JoJo meowed. "HE JUMPS OUT OF NOWHERE."

Buddy spied the area. "I KNOW. IF YOU'RE TALKING ABOUT BLITZ, I'VE RUN INTO HIM A FEW TIMES. HE LIKES TO BULLY."

Henry called Jane on his phone. "We found JoJo in the alley behind your house."

Soon, Jane joined them in the alley. "Oh my! JoJo is stuck on one of the top branches. How will she ever get down?"

JoJo meowed and clung to the limb.

Henry scanned the tree from bottom to top. "I can try to climb up to her if you have a ladder."

"Sure. I'll be right back." Jane ran to her garage.

JoJo whined, "DON'T LEAVE ME."

Buddy barked, "HOLD ON! HELP IS ON THE WAY."

Jane came back and leaned her ladder against the tree trunk.

"Here, hold Buddy's leash. I'll see what I can do." Henry began to climb.

Buddy yipped, "JOJO, HENRY WILL SAVE YOU."

Henry climbed to the top rung of the ladder. He reached for JoJo. "Here, kitty."

The trembling cat meowed and crept closer to Henry's hand. He grasped her soft body and carried her in one arm as he went back down.

"Good job," Jane cheered.

"YAY!" Buddy howled.

"Oh, JoJo, I'm so glad you're safe." Jane lifted the pretty cat from Henry's arms. "Thank you for your help. Just leave the ladder against the tree. I will take JoJo inside. I'm sure she's starving."

"I never would have found her without Buddy." Henry patted his little beagle.

Jane looked into Buddy's brown eyes. "I'm sorry. I don't have a treat for you."

The little beagle cocked his head. *No treats? Did the bandit come to your house too? How sad.*

On the way home, Henry and Buddy stopped at the dog park.

"Hi, Buddy." Max welcomed his friend to the small-dog zone. "What's new?"

Henry opened the gate and Buddy trotted inside. "I'm glad we can finally talk. Where's Willie?"

"Over by the lake. Willie said he's a big dog now. He wants to play with Blitz."

Buddy peered through the fence. "No surprise. Willie did not believe me."

"Willie said he thinks Blitz will solve the case. They think JoJo is the bandit."

Buddy sniffed closer to Max. "They want to blame JoJo without the proof. I met JoJo this morning. She said she has not stolen anything."

Blitz galloped up to the fence and howled, "Hey, you losers, the case is closed. I solved the crime."

Willie trotted close behind. "He sure did. Blitz is the Super Sleuth of Blueberry Street."

"Blitz, did you chase JoJo up a tree? You scared her," Buddy barked.

"Why shouldn't I? She's the bandit," Blitz snarled. "She'll never steal again. I've solved the case, and I've earned the title."

Buddy stepped closer to the fence. "Do you have any proof JoJo took the treats?"

Blitz barked, "She's a cat. I don't need proof."

Willie wiggled side to side. "You tell them, Blitz. Cats are no good."

Blitz barked, "What's wrong with you, Buddy? First, you save a monkey. Then, you protect a cat. What kind of dog are you? What have you done to solve the case?"

Buddy sniffed the ground near the fence. "I'm still looking. We must wait to see if any more treats are stolen before we close the case."

At home, Jen sat by Buddy on the floor. "Time to brush your teeth, little guy." She smeared the toothpaste on the brush.

Buddy rolled onto his back and opened his mouth. *Yum, I love the chicken flavor almost as much as Yummy Treats.* He stuck out his tongue to lap up all the toothpaste.

Henry glanced up from his book. "Buddy still likes doggy toothpaste."

Jen placed the cap on the tube. "Buddy, you're a good dog. We need to order more Yummy Treats. Maybe the bandit moved to a new place."

"You've got a point. I'll place another order." Henry reached for his laptop. "Great. Yummy Treats are on sale. Two for the price of one. This time, I'll order two packs to last a few weeks."

Buddy stood and wagged his tail. *Henry looks happy and I heard him say Yummy Treats. What will happen next?*

Henry closed his laptop. "All done. Our box will arrive in two days. I'm tired. Let's go to bed."

Henry tucked Buddy into his crate. "Good night."

Buddy peered into the darkness. *JoJo and Freddy climb trees and need help. If Freddy is the bandit, he steals because he's hungry. I need to help Freddy, but Henry won't let me near him. What can I do? I can't run or jump. Maybe Blitz is right when he calls me a loser. I wonder if Max will give up on me too.*

Buddy sighed and closed his eyes. Soon, he fell asleep.

CHAPTER NINE

Special Delivery

Ding Dong!

Buddy heard footsteps on the porch. *Who's at the door?*

Then, a car engine started and drove away.

Buddy perked his ears. *Now someone is trying to scoot something away from the door.* The little beagle barked.

Jen bounded down the stairs. "What's going on, Buddy? Is someone at the door?" She looked through the peephole. "I don't see anyone. Let's go into the kitchen."

Buddy didn't follow Jen. He pawed at the front door.

She picked him up and carried him away. Then, she closed the doggy gate.

Buddy paced the floor. *I have a strange feeling, Jen.*

All of a sudden, Henry walked in the back door. "Hey, I got a text saying our package came."

"Oh, I heard Buddy bark. I looked through the peephole, but I didn't see anyone. Why don't you check the front porch?"

Henry opened the front door. "Oh, no!"

Jen and Buddy hurried to the foyer. "What happened?"

"Our package of Yummy Treats arrived. But the box is torn and half of the treats are gone. I think the bandit couldn't carry this heavy box."

Jen grabbed Buddy's collar. "Well, at least we still have treats. You were smart to place a big order."

Buddy wagged his tail. *Yay! More Yummy Treats for me.*

Henry carried the tattered box inside. "Whoever opened the box might return. I have an idea."

Buddy pawed Henry's leg. *Hey, don't forget me. Do you have a treat for me? I'm still here.*

"Oh, sorry, Bud. I forgot about you." Henry gave his beagle the tasty prize.

Buddy gulped and licked his lips. *Heavenly.*

Henry found an empty brown box in the garage. He wrapped some Yummy Treats inside and taped the carton shut.

Buddy cocked his head. *Are you saving those treats for me?*

Henry picked up his phone. "Charlie, this is Henry. Can you come over? I need to tell you about my plan."

Soon, Charlie rang the doorbell. Jen greeted Charlie and Max. "We've been expecting you. How about a cup of coffee?"

"Sure." Charlie took off Max's leash.

Buddy yipped, "HI, MAX. IF YOU ARE GOOD, HENRY MIGHT GIVE YOU A TREAT. HE GAVE ME ONE THIS MORNING. I'LL SHOW YOU HOW TO BEHAVE LIKE A GOOD DOG."

Max wagged his tail. "YOU HAVE TREATS? THANKS FOR INVITING ME."

Buddy and Max watched Henry as he sat at the kitchen table with Jen and Charlie.

Henry sipped his coffee. "The postman set my big order of Yummy Treats on the porch today. The thief stole some Yummy Treats but left a few inside. I think the bandit is too small to carry much."

Charlie spooned some sugar into his cup. "Small? Do you think a raccoon stole our treats? They've been seen by the garbage cans."

Henry gazed out the window. "A raccoon is possible, I suppose. They will eat anything."

Jen noticed Max and Buddy. "Look at our dogs. They're watching us."

Henry reached into his pocket and tossed each beagle a treat.

Buddy gulped. "SEE, I TOLD YOU. WORKS EVERY TIME."

Max licked his lips. "I LIKE LEARNING HOW TO BEHAVE LIKE A GOOD DOG, BUDDY."

Henry reached for the brown box on the table. "Let's set a trap. I put treats in this box. Charlie, take this box to your car. Drive home and then come back to our house. You can act like the postman. Set the box on my porch and ring the doorbell."

Charlie nodded. "Great idea, Henry. You and Buddy can hide behind the front hedge. When I drive away, you can watch to see who comes."

"I want to help." Jen patted Max. "What if I keep Max with me? We'll hide on the side of the house and catch the bandit if needed."

"Yes." Charlie picked up the box and gazed at his pet. "Max, behave. I'll return soon."

"Good." Henry stood up. "Let's go. We must stay quiet."

CHAPTER TEN

A Furry Finale

From their hiding place behind the hedge, Buddy and Henry watched Charlie drive up. He ran from his car and placed the box of treats on the front porch. Then, he rang the bell and hopped back into the car.

Henry gasped. "I see Jane's cat."

Buddy strained his neck around the hedge. *JoJo? I didn't think she went out during the day. She can't be the bandit.*

The calico cat darted around the side of the porch and raced down Blueberry Street toward her house.

Buddy sighed. *I'm glad JoJo didn't take the box on the porch. She's a good cat.* Buddy peeked around the hedge again. Something small, brown, and furry dropped down from the roof. *Freddy the monkey?* Buddy squirmed.

Henry pulled on the leash. "Stay. I think our bandit is a wild monkey."

Freddy ran up the porch steps. He raced back down with the box of Yummy Treats in one hand.

Buddy lunged from the hedge and howled, "Stop!"

Max rushed from the side of the house. The two beagles blocked Freddy's path to the street and howled nonstop.

Freddy was afraid and climbed to the roof still holding the box of treats under his arm. The little monkey frowned. "Hi, Buddy."

Buddy barked, "I know you're hungry, Freddy, but stealing is wrong. Those treats do not belong to you."

Soon, neighbors gathered to see the event.

"The beagles cornered the bandit," Charlie said. He went to the porch and grabbed Max's leash.

The crowd pointed when a larger monkey appeared on the roof.

The adult monkey chattered, "Son, I've looked all over for you."

"Mama!" The wild baby rushed to his mother for a hug. "I got lost."

Mama monkey scolded Freddy. "What do you have in your hand?"

"I've been hungry," Freddy chattered.

Mama monkey wagged her finger in Freddy's face. "Remember, I told you not to steal."

Buddy barked, "Those were my Yummy Treats."

Mama monkey peered down from the roof. "Buddy, I'm sorry Freddy stole your treats." She turned to Freddy. "You must give them back, son."

Then, Blitz and Doug joined the group in front of the house. Blitz panted. "I've chased JoJo up and down Blueberry Street. The fur ball got away. What's going on here?"

"Look up." Buddy lifted his head toward the roof. "Max and I caught the bandit. His name is Freddy and he's a wild monkey."

Blitz barked, "What an ugly animal."

"You're a bully, Blitz. I think he's cute," Buddy yipped.

"Are you sure Freddy is the bandit? What proof do you have?" Blitz growled.

"Look in his hand." Buddy wagged his tail.

Mama monkey reached for the treats, but Freddy stepped back and fell to the ground.

"Oh no!" Freddy's mama scurried down from the roof. She picked up her baby and rocked him in her arms.

Freddy chattered, "I'm okay, Mama."

Two agents arrived with a net. One said, "Step back, everyone. Let us through."

The men spread the net over the wild monkeys. They carried the animals to a cage in the back of their truck.

One of them spoke to the crowd. "Don't worry, everyone. We're from Florida Wildlife. Your neighbor, Jen, called us."

Jen stepped forward. "I am Jen."

"Thank you for helping us save these animals. They must have left their home in Sapphire Springs. We will take them farther south. Evershade National Park gives them more space to run free and find food."

The crowd cheered and the men drove off.

Buddy watched the truck drive away. "I GUESS I WON'T SEE FREDDY ANYMORE."

Max yipped, "BUDDY, DON'T BE SAD. YOU SOLVED THE CASE. YOU'RE THE SUPER SLEUTH OF BLUEBERRY STREET."

"WHO'S THE BANDIT?" Willie wiggled his way through the crowd. "I FOLLOWED JOJO ALL DAY, BUT SHE HAS NO TREATS."

"SORRY, WILLIE," Blitz sighed. "BUDDY HAS PROOF OF MONKEY BUSINESS. HE CAN'T RUN, BUT HE CAN FIND CLUES. HE CAUGHT THE BANDIT AND EARNED THE TITLE OF SUPER SLEUTH."

Buddy wagged his tail. "YOU HELPED, MAX. WITH MY NOSE AND YOUR FEET, WE MAKE A GREAT TEAM."

Charlie moved through the crowd. "I found a box of Yummy Treats in the yard. Are these yours, Henry?"

Henry grasped the bag. "Thank you. The baby monkey dropped the box when he fell from the roof. Now we can give treats to our dogs. Come, my four-legged friends. Yummy Treats for all."

A few weeks later, Henry parked their trailer at Evershade National Park. He lifted the back gate of the jeep. "We're here."

Henry and Buddy walked around the campground.

Buddy kept his nose to the sand. *I smell a wild monkey.* He looked for the highest tree. A monkey sat on the top branch. *I see Freddy.*

The little monkey waved, grabbed a vine, and swung away into the woods.

Buddy sighed. *Freddy has plenty to eat in his new home. I'm glad he's happy and free.*

Henry tugged on the leash. "What do you see, boy?"

Buddy smiled his doggy smile. *I see a happy ending.*

QUESTIONS FOR DISCUSSION

1. Buddy and Max had trouble following the rules when they were no longer rewarded with treats. Would you obey your parents and teachers if you did not receive a reward?

2. Blitz and Willie thought JoJo was the bandit because "all cats are bad." Explain what might happen if we falsely blame others. Has anyone blamed you for something you did not do? How did you feel?

3. How did Blitz affect Buddy's self-confidence? Who encouraged Buddy? Who encourages you? Do you encourage others?

4. Teamwork is important when a community is trying to solve a problem. Which characters worked well together?

5. Buddy learned Freddy was lost, hungry, and needed help. As cities grow, animal habitats shrink. How can we protect wild animals?

The Doggone Truth

Several hundred rhesus macaque monkeys live in the Florida Wilderness. For more information, visit the Florida Fish and Wildlife Commission at myfwc. com.

ABOUT THE AUTHOR

Debbie Burton began writing after she retired from teaching. Debbie's first book in the Tails of Blueberry Street series, *Buddy the Beagle on Blueberry Street*, was released by Elk Lake Publishing in 2019. An award-winning poet, Debbie's work has appeared in issues of *Time of Singing Literary Journal* and *Refresh Bible Study Magazine*.

Debbie is a member of Word Weavers International and SCBWI. She enjoys camping and hiking in her home state of Florida with her husband Herb and their beagle, Buddy.

Visit the author's website at debbieburton. blog. Readers can also follow Debbie and Buddy at facebook.com/buddyfanclub. If you enjoyed *Return to Blueberry Street*, please submit a review on Amazon or Goodreads.

Debbie's other Book

Buddy the Beagle on Blueberry Street

Buddy

Made in USA - North Chelmsford, MA
1177390_9781649490476
10.08.2020 1618